The Appalachian Trail Tells a Tale

The Appalachian Trail is more than geography that extends through 14 states and 2200 miles of challenging terrain. For poet Gary Drury, his nonfiction account of his rendezvous with Mother Nature, or, as he describes her, a "cruel, relentless mistress," the Appalachian Trail represented an epic journey. Drury is not a camper. Not a hiker. Not a backpacker, boulder scrambler, athlete, or rock climber. In order to embark on the journey that he undertook in 2014, he says, "I elected to step 180 degrees outside my comfort zone." He began the journey as a novice. By the end, he realized that he had undergone a life-changing event.

But he's a poet. So it was perhaps inevitable that he would turn the images into words when the journey ended. He's writing about his experiences, including the episode where he was nearly carried out in a body bag, and found the physical death to be reaffirming. The journey began, Drury admits, under romantic impressions he gleaned from a National Geographic documentary. There were times when he questioned why he was subjecting himself to the physical ordeal. He was too stubborn to give up. But just as powerful as his determination was his dedication to the deceased family members he honored with his quest, and the chari-

"Risky" Business

Photos Taken by:
Top: A.T. Conservatory personal.
Bottom Left: "Angie", Bottom Right: "Texas"

Scale To NEW HEIGHTS!

The Drury Gazette Staff
Gary Drury, Author / Editor / Journalist / Minister / Publisher

© 2016 by Gary Drury / The Drury Gazette

Contact Information: No Phone Calls Accepted without prior appointment. For expedited correspondence please visit www.druryspublishing.com.

Serious inquiries ONLY, please. Spammers will be reported to their ISPs, authorities and legal action may ensue.

The Drury Gazette promotes raising authors. Its a non-profit private corporation sole ministry encourages strong Christian values, defends and supports inalienable rights, The Republic-United States of America Constitution: freedoms of press, religion & speech, etc. ***26 U.S. Code § 508 (c) (1) (A).** Gifts are tax deductible.

You can direct individuals interested in The Drury Gazette to www.druryspublishing.com to download a FREE issue. Enjoy!

WINTER 2016

Issue 1 Volume 10

ISBN-13: 978-0692658420

ISSN: 1930-0875 (Print)
ISSN: 1930-0883 (PDF)

Gary Drury, Editor/Publisher. Established in 1982, Promotes well-grounded moral and spiritual values of all beliefs and faiths. I am devoted to creative expression and free speech. Correspondence, submissions, supportive donations and subscriptions should be directed to the publisher.

The Drury Gazette © ™ by Gary Drury Ministries © ™
www.druryspublishing.com © ™

NON-PROFIT QUARTERLY PUBLICATION
508 (c) (1) (A)

Cover photo, design, and layout by Gary Drury © ™

Printed in The Republic-United States of America.

00
ISSN 1930-0875

9 771930 087003 >

00
ISSN 1930-0883

9 771930 088000 >

Contents

ties, including the Red Cross, St. Jude's, and the Salvation Army that he supported with his hiking.

He got the idea from fellow hikers who, as they shared their experiences, told Drury that he should put his in print. "My memories, experiences, socialization will last a lifetime." He answered with warm inviting smile and a campfire glow gleaming in his slate-gray eyes. The working title of his book <u>MY FEET ON FIRE</u> will surely inspire others to seek adventure of their own, perhaps endeavor a journey of the Appalachian Trail.

Not everyone is going to hike the Appalachian Trail. Not everyone wants to, not everyone is able to. But for those who would like to experience the journey vicariously, walking the Trail in Drury's footsteps as they read his words, the book will be a travel guide. Drury's book <u>MY FEET ON FIRE</u> can take you to the Trail, where you'll share the struggles and the triumphs of seven months that Drury, battered in body and exultant in spirit, will always remember.

Drury speculates his book will be available sometimes in 2016/2017. He extends a special thank you to all the hikers that made his trek unique, genuine and wonderful during his most trying moments.

Visit

regularly for updates.

Photos Taken by:
Top: "Fyr Fly"
Right: "Angie's friend"

GRANDMA'S SUNBONNET QUILT

Iva and Eva pieced it from flour sacks
back in the winter of 1888

they trimmed hundreds of material slices
then sewed them

together in the kerosened halo
through blizzard-blanketed Kansas nights

their precise stitches
marching in three-fourths inch time

through three generations
those threads have
come to spread
into my life
to hold me together

now

— © Sheryl L. Nelms

EDWIN A. NELMS

the quick flick of a smile
is still there
the curly hair still
coal black
at 67

the luminous brown
eyes softer now
mellowed
by the Valium

and the body
like a wool sweater
washed in hot water

shrunk
from six foot two
down to five foot four
bones
poke out
under his skin

his shriveled bottom
hangs in his slacks
like a limp
beanbag

brittle bone
cancer

has turned him
into a crisp cicada shell
ready to crunch
if I hug him

— © Sheryl L. Nelms

DAVE'S READY

the new clothes
are ready
and laid out

the little rag rug
is bought

he has all of the supplies
on the list
crayons
thick pencil #2
A Big Chief
rounded scissors
and glue all sacked
up to go

it's all there

he's met the teacher
and she's pretty
he's seen his room
they have hamsters
and guppies

it will be fun
he knows

now if I
can just let him

go

— © **Sheryl L. Nelms**

WHAT I AM

I have stood for many years,
providing a needed retreat
for those who sit beneath me
to escape the summertime heat.

I stretch my long and wooden arms
to meet the shining sun,
and offer birds a place to land
when a new day has begun.

In the summer the gown I wear
is colored verdant green,
but when the winter snow falls down
my gown looks crystalline.

I guard the forest every day
and greet the birds that fly,
asking them to visit me
as they go flitting by.

As I look upon the land
my heart fills up with glee
for I have lasted many years
as a mighty tall oak tree.

— © **Sheila B. Roark**

RAIN

The day wears hues of charcoal gray
from clouds that float on by,
blocking out the golden sun
that hides high in the sky.

Birds are deep within the trees
protected from the rain
waiting for the sun to shine
and warm them up again.

It is a time to rest a while
as they sit in the trees,
a time when rain drops gently fall
upon the blowing breeze.

Throughout the day the droplets fall
far from the sky above,
a blessing sent to quench the earth,
a gift from God above.

— © Sheila B. Roark

LOVERS WALK THE BEACH

Pristine sand kissed by the waves
shines with a brilliant light
sent down from a shiny sun
so golden and so bright.

Sea Gulls dance upon the waves
and ride the gentle tides
looking for a bite to eat
enjoying nature's ride.

On this torrid summer day
as gulls fly in the air
two young lovers holding hands
speak of the life they'll share.

So, on this day of sharing love
they walk upon the sand
vowing they will always stay
as they hold each others hand.

— © Sheila B. Roark

TOGETHER AGAIN

The sisters used to be so close
growing and learning each day,
but when they grew up they decided
to live their lives far, far away.

They were too busy to visit their father
the man who chased all of their fears,
the man who loved them with all of his heart
and spent time wiping their tears.

When the Cancer was found by the doctors
attacking him both day and night
his daughters came back to be with him
to help him be strong and to fight.

Once again they were gathered together
supporting their weak and sick dad
talking about the times that they shared
and all of the love that they had.

So, as they watch him get sicker
and fade from their wet, heavy eyes,
they lean on each other to keep going
as they mourn their sweet father's demise.

The girls quietly wait by his bedside
praying that he will not die,
but knowing the time is approaching
when he'll say his final goodbye.

— © Sheila B. Roark

Flames of Mame is a story of a very wealthy man and women who are married and lived in the mid 1800 hundreds and have had to be apart approximately 12 years due to extreme circumstances beyond their control. She being of an Aristocratic family with status and money and him being very rich in his own right.

Flames of Mame weaves in out of the years of separation and their deep affectionate love for each other, how their story brought about an even deeper change in their life styles they had previously lived and known.

Flames of Mame is in an Era of politics emerging, the War, the times of rebuilding war torn South and North, a time of restoring communities and lives. Becoming totally different from whom you were born as, who you have become, by worldly circumstances and changes of your life styles and gathering the hope of Love, and Reunion in a uncharted territory neither expected to find themselves in.

Juliet R. Lynch NEW BOOK **Flames of Mame**, Drury Publishing, Paperback, Pages, Retail $14.99, **ISBN-10:** 0615899528, **ISBN-13:** 978-0615899527 You will find it available wherever fine books are sold. Check with your local book store or favorite online bookstore.

Palm Sunday is a saga about an Italian American family growing up in Brooklyn. The story follows the adventures of this large warm family as they move from Brooklyn to New Jersey and some as far as Florida. However, no matter how far the family is flung from each other they gather each Palm Sunday and Christmas to celebrate the holiday and more importantly the family. The story centers on five female cousins and how they grow and prosper-their loves, joys, and sorrows. The story moves between the present time and the past telling of their parents and grandparents and how the family came to this country. The story concerns the grandparents and parents and their lives and fortunes and the children who in turn grow to have children and even grandchildren of their own. Each Palm Sunday and Christmas the family members reconnect and join together sharing their lives.

Palm Sunday
ISBN-10: 0-9770533-9-3
ISBN-13: 978-0-9770533-9-1
Pages: 64 Trim Size: 6" x 9"

Checkout Paperback & Digital Copies
Smoke Gets In Your Eyes, **The Highway Man**, **The Gypsy Fortuneteller**, **Profusion Of Lilacs**, **Museums**, **Giverny**, **Early Scenes of a Marriage**, **A Society of Two**, **Are They Winning?**

Susan C. Barto (Book Reviewer)is a regular contributor to several anthologies, magazines and gazettes and has authored seven books. Barto's books available online and bookstores.

Editor's Choice Award Winner

BETTY LOU HEBERT

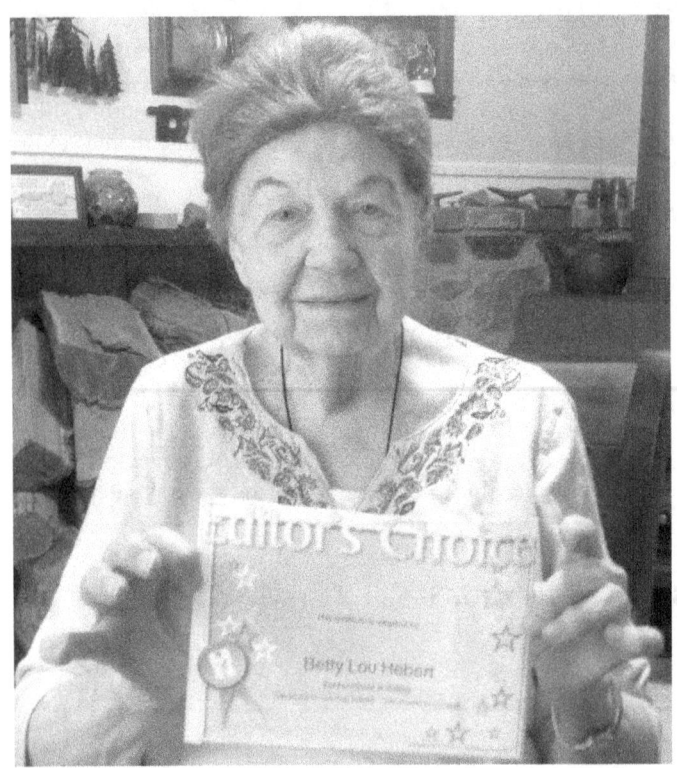

Betty lives in the country of north Idaho, with her handicapped son. They enjoy life there, the natural surroundings and all the beautiful wildlife they see. She is a widower and has two older offspring who are happily married. Betty has been writing plethora years, it brings her great joy and inner peace. Her love for writing began around age ten, she has been writing steadily the past fifteen plus years. Her myriad interests are varied. Betty loves traveling, reading, writing, working on craft projects, gardening, cooking, and enjoys a multitude of music genres. Not surprisingly, Betty is assembling the wealth of her vast writings into a wonderful collection of poetry that should be available in 2017.

Book Reviews by Susan C. Barto

A STRING OF PEARLS by Marion H. Youngquist is a novel about the Greatest Generation that takes the reader from the depression through World War II. The story is told through the eyes and experiences of a young girl named Anna Marie Schultz whom we first meet as an eight-year-old. We travel along with Anna through this history-making years and experience this time with her.

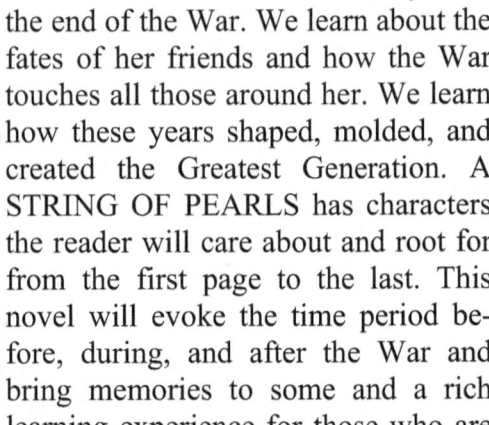

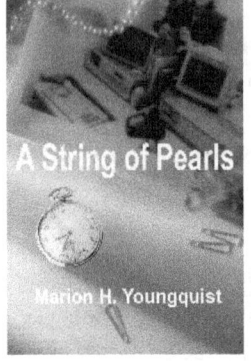

We meet her brave mother who is bringing up Anna with the help of her brother and without Anna's father. We don't learn the story of Anna's birth and the mystery surrounding it until deep into the novel. Anna is blessed with not only her strong mother but her wise and compassionate uncle. Anna takes us through the depression years where she learns thrift and enjoys life without luxuries but full of love and caring.

We follow Anna and her friends and family into World War II from Pearl Harbor Day until the end of the War. We learn about the fates of her friends and how the War touches all those around her. We learn how these years shaped, molded, and created the Greatest Generation. A STRING OF PEARLS has characters the reader will care about and root for from the first page to the last. This novel will evoke the time period before, during, and after the War and bring memories to some and a rich learning experience for those who are too young to remember.

Susan C. Barto (Book Reviewer) is a regular contributor to several magazines and gazettes and has authored seven books. Barto's books available online and bookstores.

COLOR MY SOUL, a book of poetry written by poetic artist Gary Drury, paints the soul with colors of love: Love of God, Love of Nature, Love of man for woman. The poetry is colored with all the shades and hues of love in all its forms. Some of the forms are tortured—one poem refers to Edgar Allen Poe and consequently is dark. However, the book sings about love with joyous abandon.

The books are artistic in its abstract form very like a painting. In the poem MY AMUSEMENT about Poe the artist mourns the lack of color in despair where life is like a masquerade. The poems celebrate God and nature and sometimes, again as in the Poe poem flirt with suicide. As the poet celebrates love in all its forms he, in turn, expresses pain and sorrow caused by love. The poet struggles with ecstasy, guilt, pain, and tender emotions in tandem. Sometimes he seems to feel sinfulness associated with loving while at other times he seems to feel in concert with God and nature.

The poet writes about physical love and spiritual love sometimes as though they could be in conflict. He enjoys sensuous touch and heartfelt adoration. The poet is mesmerized and then awakened out of darkness into the light carrying the reader along on his journey toward love's fulfillment.

COLOR MY SOUL, ISBN: 1-4137-6977-2 Available in Bookstores Now! Get your copy of Color My Soul by Gary Drury, ISBN: 1-4137-6977-2, Size: 6 x 9, Pages: 80. Save $'s when you buy direct. To place your order call: 1.240.529.1031

Available everywhere fine books are SOLD.

CANDLE IN THE WIND is a poetry collection about God and love. The poems celebrate the Lord's goodness and show how he guides our lives. The poems show hope and faith that abound with the belief in our Lord.

Some poems tell about our angels, our Guardian angels and all Heaven's angels who come to us with help and point the way to enrich our lives. The poems glorify God and give us the hope of the Resurrection and the Second Coming.

The poems talk about how the love of the Lord can color and enrich our lives. Like a Candle in the Wind the light of our Lord can show us the path to take.

One poem is in praise of the beautiful four seasons of the year that color our world. One poem describes a garden and others speak of hope even in the face of the death and mourning of our departed loved ones.

This collection of Gary Drury's newest poems should not be missed. It will enrich your library of poetry.

CANDLE IN THE WIND List Price: $14.99 6" x 9" (15.24 x 22.86 cm) Black & White on White paper,158 pages , ISBN-13: 978-1440475207, ISBN-10: 1440475202

Susan C. Barto (Book Reviewer) a regular contributor to several magazines & gazettes, has authored several books.

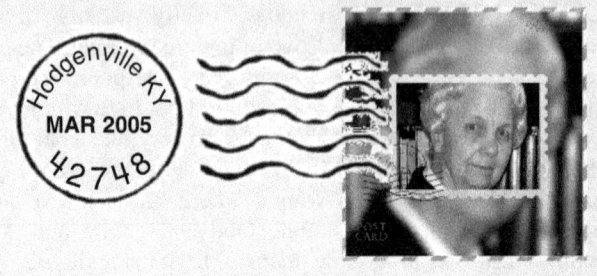

Procula
by Marion H. Youngquist
Celebrating 10th Anniversary 2005 - 2015

Avid readers dive into the Roman era of history and mystery. PROCULA novel sports a wealth of researched historical facts intertwined with mystery and intrigue surrounding Pontius Pilate's wife PROCULA.

Set in Biblical times, Procula. a young girl, is raised by wealthy relatives in Rome. She marries Pontius Pilate, an Army officer, who is sent to Palestine as Emperor Tiberius' personal representative to "keep the peace". When Jesus (a popular Jewish rabbi from Nazareth) is jailed, Procula warns Pilate against involvement. He ignores her. Later, Pilate is summoned to Rome on false charges, but Procula manages their escape. This adventure story, based on historical research, recreates Biblical personalities. Born in a remote village, little is known of this woman until now. The world will never know how her influence could have altered the course of history. See how her own trials and tribulations influenced her life. And later positioned her into a seat of great power as wife to Pontius Pilate. Read for yourself as you take this remarkable journey into ancient Palestine to watch her life unfold. A sophisticated woman of means taunted by powerful imagery in her dreams. When a situation unfolded before Pilate, his wife quickly advised him to be cautious. Had she been more persistent, she may have been able to arrest the crucifixion. Later this caring woman of influence and power seeks sanctuary with her family in AEgyptus, in a small obscure city where they lived under assumed names. Isn't it time you discover the woman who may have changed history?

Enter to Win a FREE Copy of PROCULA

Marion H. Youngquist was born and educated in Salem, Oregon. She was a news reporter in Oregon and Nebraska where she graduated from Midland Lutheran College, Fremont, She also studied at Coe College, Cedar Rapids, IA, UW-Milwaukee, and seminars in Europe. She *scribbles* on planes, ships and in airports--gathering dialog and situations she overhears. For ten years she was a synodical editor and correspondent for The Lutheran and a contributor to other magazines. For ten years she was a synodical editor and correspondent for The Lutheran and a contributor to other magazines. She has written plays for Wauwatosa Village Playhouse. Two full-length plays--The Distlefink and The Gift-Givers--have won prizes as well as her poetry. A poem, Fourth of July Night, was included in a 12-month song cycle by composer Charyl Zehfus. Youngquist also co-authored Little Critters, a children's musical, with Lorraine Brugh, composer, published by Contemporary Drama Service. Procula is her first historical novel, (about the wife of Pontius Pilate) officially released by Drury's Publishing, August 2005. She belongs to the Wisconsin Fellowship of Poets, the Council for Wisconsin Writers, Tuesday A.M. Poets--Milwaukee, and The Dramatists Guild of America. Youngquist and her husband Ted, a retired Lutheran minister, live in Wauwatosa, WI. They have four children, six grandchildren (another deceased), and three great-granddaughters."

Your Advertisement Could Be HERE!?

Mark Stoll's chapbooks and CD's *(Use this order form or a photocopy.)*

ORDER FORM

Name: _____
Address: _____
City: _____
State: _____
Zip: _____
Phone: _____

TITLE	PRICE		QTY	SUB TOTAL
"Rhythm and Rhyme"	@ $6.00 ea.	X	____	$ _____
"More Rhythm More Rhyme"	@ $6.00 ea.	X	____	$ _____
"It's a Coffee House Thing"	@ $6.00 ea.	X	____	$ _____
"Verbal Abuse"	@ $6.00 ea.	X	____	$ _____
"Don't Judge This Book by its Cover"	@ $6.00 ea.	X	____	$ _____
"Stoll Stories"	@ $6.00 ea.	X	____	$ _____
"MS more stuff by Mark Stoll"	@ $6.00 ea.	X	____	$ _____
"Mark Stoll, Acoustic" CD	@ $12.00 ea.	X	____	$ _____

Grand Total Due $ _____

Make check or money order payable and mailed to:

Mark Stoll
P.O.Box 24212
Columbus, Ohio 43224

Postage will be paid by addressee. Please allow four to six weeks for delivery. Do not send cash.

Thank you for your order.

KEEPER OF THE PAST

I still plant new flowers every spring
And wait for colored promises they bring.
I search to find the first star of the night
And make a wish upon it's twinkling light.
Although I know that nothing stays the same,
Still, I won't let the wind forget your name.
I'll keep alive the lovely songs we sang,
Remembering the way our voices rang.
And I will act in days still left tome,
As keeper of the way things used to be.

— © **Betty Lou Hebert**

UNTITLED

Simmering in my own emotional juices,
trying to communicate what I am feeling
ain't easy.
Isolated, words don't seem to convey
the necessary nuance.
Maybe I'll play a song
that expresses my state.
It's better than the blah-blah,
trying to express myself,
ending up with an awkward detail.

— © **Milton Kerr**

CREATIVITY

Why do we create
the things we do?
Could it be imagination
in high gear revved up
from low gear of necessity?
Perhaps we create things
simply because we can.
Is divinity a prime factor
involved to advance the
human race to a higher
plane of existence, or
could it be persistence
to achieve things to
eliminate boredom
of a humdrum life,
rife with strife of
wanting things better
and different than
what they are?
Is inspiration simply
yearning for freedom?
How far can we go
without knowing any
boundaries to restrict
us from going insane
by not creating anything
at all, would we be in
the cauldron of nothingness?
I guess it is time
to let philosophy class
101 recess for the
duration of summer!
I bid you all adieu!

"What is inspiration?
It is everything the eye
hath seen, the ear hath
heard, the heart hath
felt; it is a kaleidoscope
on the carousel of soul!"

— © **Gerald Heyder**

REFLECTIONS

We are but scholars of our past,
Mirrors of the lessons of age,
Reflecting the smiles and sighs
Upon a twilight page.

There is no turning back,
The moment passes on;
We have a choice but once
And then the time is gone.

We could have gifted flowers,
Been quicker with a hand,
Shared more tears of grief
To show we understand.

We learn most from our errors
In the trials of don't and do
And the Master tallies all
When the final course is through.

So forgive mistakes of youth,
And care not about the score,
We meant to do our best --
No one can ask for more.

— © **C. David Hay**

A MAN FROM DAKOTA

Within the precinct house there sat
A homeless man with battered hat.
His eyes were gazing at the past.
The sorrow in his features cast
A shaft of sympathy for one
Who felt his life was nearly done.

His name was Bill and he had come
From North Dakota. That's the sum
Of knowledge he supplied and yet,
Somehow we never could forget
The haunted eyes, the hopeless air,
That emanated from him there.

An officer, with camera came
And verified this transient's name.
Then took a picture, capturing,
The essence of Bill's wandering
And when enlarged, it had appeal.
Emotions shown were so real.

It hung awhile up on display
And everyone who passed that way,
Was taken by the quality.
The great despair that all could see.
But now, it hangs upon our wall.
A homeless man, home, after all!

— © **Betty Lou Hebert**

Fresh Memories

I remember days upon the dunes,
Where the ocean sang us salty tunes!
We hiked and sat to stare at all the sand
And hold the warmth of it within a hand.
It sifted through our fingers just like time.
We weren't aware, for being in our prime,
But now in looking back I wonder why
We didn't know that life was passing by!
How different our days then might have been
If for a single moment we had seen
How brief those carefree hours on the shore.
How many years would pass again before
I'd find myself in that same place and see
That being there alone was misery!
Yet I still cling to memories that stay
As fresh as though they took place yesterday!

— © Betty Lou Hebert

Sedgwick County Juvenile Officer

In memory of my father

He always worried about his kids

the runaways who traveled hell
before he found them
the beaten children

the two-year-old he talked about
for days wondered how
a mother could do that
to her own baby

the neglected kids

he cried once for the eight kids
he found living in a miniature house
with seven dogs and rooms full of flies
and dog shit and a bottle of Ketchup

the sexually used kids

men who did that to children
made him mad enough to kill
he said very slowly

in the kids he had hope
always said there was no
such thing as a bad kid

he gave them his best
until he got ulcers and a nervous break down

but his kids always came first

— © Sheryl L. Nelms

Box People

they live in cardboard boxes

they survive
the New York winter
in corrugated cubes
laid out on the sidewalks

there's old Charlie
with his snaggle-toothed
smile and four layers
of crusty clothes

head poked
up

out of his suite
of telescoping boxes

he tells how
it really
Is

even at twelve below

tells the story of
poor old Jake

"Who drank too much
Mogan David,
sweet Jesus

Didn't even make it back to his
box and a city street crew
had to pry him off
of the cement
with a shovel
Dear Lord

It's a tough life,"
he says.

— © Sheryl L. Nelms

Fighting the War Again

driving across the New Mexico desert

through the scrub cedar and pinion
up and down
the sandy hills
of Highway ninety-nine

the cancer gnarled
man beside me
a survivor of
New Caledonia
and Bouganville
of Luzon
and the Million-Dollar Tree
of sharks
and bullets
and mine fields

re-lives that war

until we believe

we see
New Zealand
and the Philippines
the squalor in
the troop-ships

feel the seasickness

and the fear
as the ship left
for Japan

feel the awe
when he
saw
The Bomb

and I wonder

— © Sheryl L. Nelms

LOVELY AUTUMN

In Autumn Tree's Become Slowly Unclothed
Season of Pumpkin Picking,
Lawns Decorated with
Scarecrows, Hot Apple Pie,
Goblins and Ghosts
Football Goal Posts
Up to the Attic Warm Sweaters Needed Now
Holiday Season Approaching
Lots to Do ***and How ***
Prepare for the Chilly Shivering Days
Frost and Snow Check Car and
Tires Ready to Go
Squirrels Gathering Food for Their Family Meal
Crisp Fall Air Makes Doing Chores
Easy with Zeal
Toasting Marshmallows around a
Field Fire after
A Soccer Game
Autumn Can Also Be Described as
Getting on in Years
Age Is How You Feel Don't Shed Tears
The Loss of an Hour by Setting Clocks to
Climb Can't
Diminish the Elegant, Artistic Sculpture
Of Autumn Time

— © **Sandra Glassman**

SEASONS OF LONG LIFE

The warmth in the budding of Springtime
melts more than the snow on the street
green grass, blooming trees, early sunrise
combine to make what you're feeling complete.
The bright sun eventually grows heavy
so intensified before Summers end
you anticipate the sun-set in the evening
when the gentle breeze
becomes your best friend.

Autumn rushes in to splash color
on the myriad of fast, falling leaves
with beauty that is so breathtaking
precedes the inevitable Winter freeze.
This season so harsh and demanding
will arrive to strike it's death blow
the cold, north wind soon is howling
it brings a blanket of pure, pristine snow.

Your life is in the changing of seasons
these truths you will find to be true
you don't know which one you'll be living
when seasons end time arrives just for you.
Springtime brought you joy to be living
to pursue all your Summertime dreams
you labored long to secure your rich Autumn
for a blessed rest as the Wintertime deems.

Will your harvest be enough to sustain you
in the precious time where you now abide
is the fire there still brightly burning
to keep you warm while the freeze is outside?
You're truly blessed if you are content there
from all the seasons that you have lived through
you can appreciate all of God's goodness
his gracious gift, a seasoned life given... to you.

— © **Janet Goven**

WILL YOU BE THERE?

During gray and sad times
when pain invades my heart,
will you hold me in your arms
whenever teardrops start?

Will you share the challenges
we'll have to face one day,
or will you leave me all alone
to cope with skies of gray?

Will you share your love with me
until we're old and gray,
or will you say you've had enough
before you go away?

As I look into your eyes
I'm not sure what I see,
for you have put up granite walls
so filled with secrecy.

— © **Sheila B. Roark**

MARMALADE SEASON

The marmalade season has started
painting the world with bright hues,
where orange and browns can be seen
everywhere
replacing the greens and the blues.

Leaves know that winter is coming
so now they must go on their way,
dancing upon the cool autumn air
on this breezy and cool autumn day.

It is the season of orange
when nature wears bright rustic hues,
delighting the world with its beauty
sharing its bright autumn views.

— © **Sheila B. Roark**

THE GOLDEN HILLS OF AUTUMN

Before me rise the golden hills of autumn
Untouched save for the gentle hands of Nature;
Behind me the sun shines warm
To belie the touch of frost upon the breeze
As it slips through the whispering trees.
Fragrant with a hint of distant wood smoke
Which always brings back memories
And I find myself thinking of home.
Instantly I journey through time and space
To a warm and welcome familiar place—
With misty eyes I gaze into the past
Which seems to lie just beyond the hills
That stretch hazily before me.
How long I stood there I do not know
But I realized that I no longer felt
The warmth of the sun upon me
For it had dropped low in the sky
And as its radiance began to die
A final flash blazed across
the fall-colored leaves.
Overcome with a warm contentment
I turned away from the vista before me;
If not tomorrow, then someday soon,
I shall travel over the golden hills of autumn
To see what wonders lie beyond.

— © **Herbert Jerry Baker**

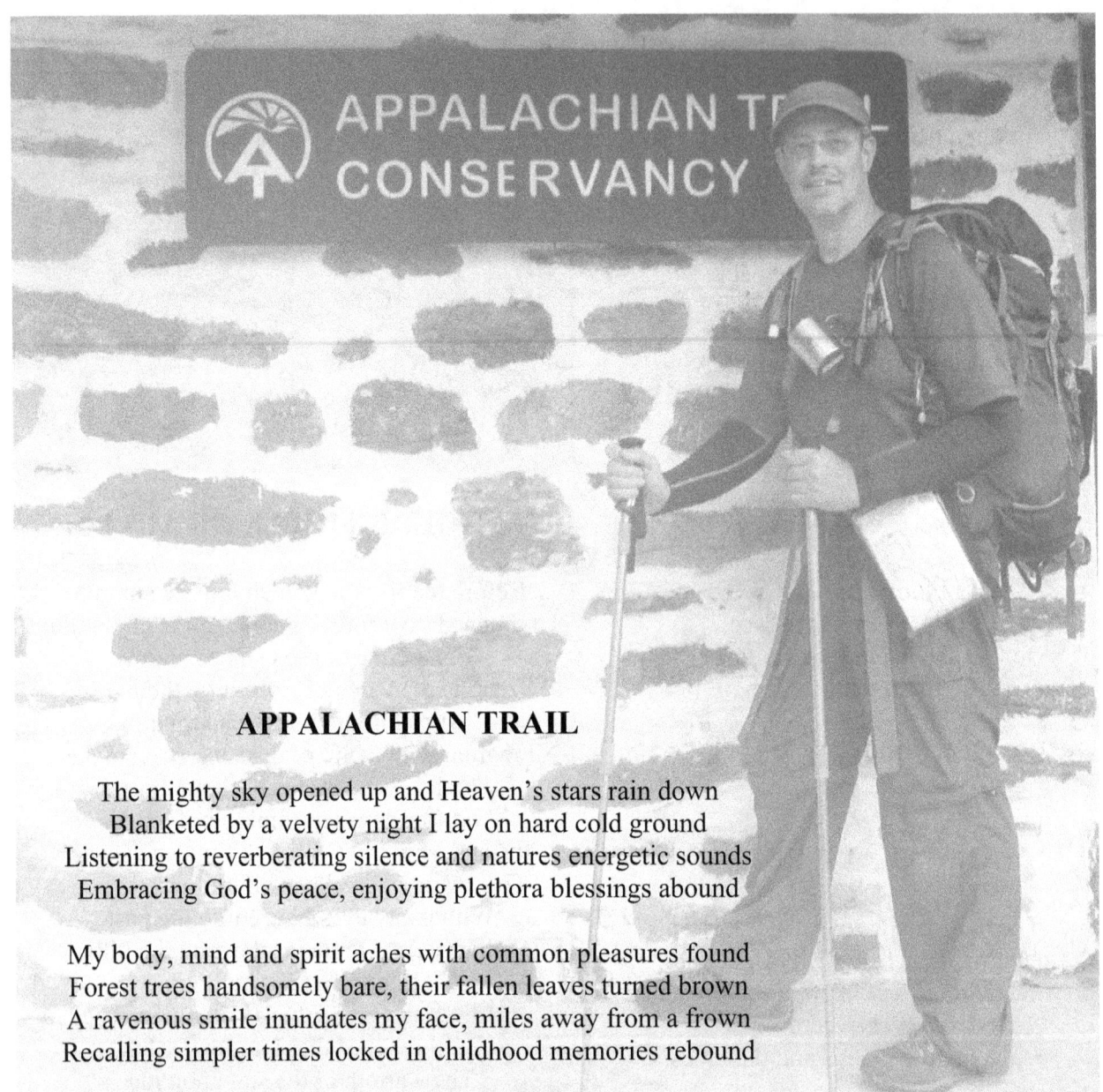

APPALACHIAN TRAIL

The mighty sky opened up and Heaven's stars rain down
Blanketed by a velvety night I lay on hard cold ground
Listening to reverberating silence and natures energetic sounds
Embracing God's peace, enjoying plethora blessings abound

My body, mind and spirit aches with common pleasures found
Forest trees handsomely bare, their fallen leaves turned brown
A ravenous smile inundates my face, miles away from a frown
Recalling simpler times locked in childhood memories rebound

This solo excursion landed me in the arms of paradise town
Proclivities crystallize my brief moment of tranquility forever now
Engrossing Irish heritage my kilt flows breezily around
Fresh fragrant morning air inflates my spirit headlong bound

Dawn is kissing darkness goodbye, my worn boots beating ground
Appalachian Trail nourishes my weary soul but I'm taking it down
Placing one foot a front the other I'm headed eagerly north bound
Sanctuary is awaiting me there, accomplishment seldom found

— © **Gary Drury**

Inspiration's Moment

When inspiration strikes bloody ink must flow
What is at stake only Heaven truly knows
God is my fire, my light, strength giving me sight
To journey onward – forward into the unknown I kite
Burying past for present, future my stone rolls
Peace eternal flame in my heart, in my soul
Resting now in natures home amidst angelic light
As canopy of gleaming stars blanket thee tonight
Day will break shortly, my trek anew, forging on I go
Burden lighter than day before as serenity has lighten my load
Masquerade of pain levels though continues to willfully bite
Mind is obstinate when flesh is strong I hike with all my might
The trajectory can be bitterly cruel where rushing streams flow,
Romancing a dream laden with thorns, slumber dusk be cold
Testicular fortitude sheds fears mask discarding all fright
I will not waver regardless of what crawls and bits with delight
Inspiration's moment of enlightenment is a live theatrical show
As character in this game of chess each step precisely slow,
Gentle signs of rebirth invigorate fortitude extinguishing plight
The wonders of nature's such a magnificent glorious bountiful hike

— © **Gary Drury**

21

BEFORE SUNSET I FEEL
THE POPLAR'S SCENT

Before sunset I feel the poplar's scent,
A familiar odor with an acrid bitterness…
Sometimes our life is opulent,
Occasionally we are in painful distress.
Oh life, how changeable is your face,
And yours forms alter the coming light.
Recently you were charming grace,
Now you appear like perpetual night.
Are you from Heaven or
from the depths of hell?
Show me that place from whence I came,
Tell me the whole truth, tell me, tell!
Why do you play a double game?

— © Adolf P. Shvedchikov, PhD

OUR LIFE IS A MIXTURE
OF HOPE AND FEAR

Our life is a mixture of hope and fear.
We pray in the night when clouds conceal
the moon,
We pray to God in the afternoon,
And have faith that despair will disappear.
Yes, we still trust, when we are in tears,
We wait that they will be the tears of joy,
Than our troubles nothing but toy,
We still believe in God and blissful years…

— © Adolf P. Shvedchikov, PhD

MY DREAMS ARE FLOATING
IN THE OCEAN

My dreams are floating in the ocean
Nonstop, every day and night,
The winds frolic and pursue their flight,
And give me bliss of new emotions.
I hear the spiritual song,
My each motive, motion, and tone
Perfectly sounds in unison.
Oh, life is charmed, nothing is wrong!

— © Adolf P. Shvedchikov, PhD

I LIKE THE WINGED WINDS
WHICH FLOW

I like the winged winds which flow.
I hear them, and once more they are mute.
They are witnesses of my long-term solitude,
They are my friends to whom I say: hello!
In essence, we need a few with a native taste:
A modest house on a sunny hill,
The china caps, an ancient coffee-mill…
For goodness sake!
Why must my time go to waste?
To be submerged into silence without sound,
Like a blooming spring in the rays of sun,
Oh mother-earth, I am your exiled son,
I'm solitary one, but our bosoms are bound…

— © Adolf P. Shvedchikov, PhD

WALKING IN THE MIDST OF EARTHLY ANGELS

by Juliet Rhodes Lynch

The sweet spirits of people who walk amongst us. The ones who walk and listen with the intent of knowing you, and enjoying your company. The voice of kindness and the endearing thought of sharing emotions, and feeling the deepest of friendships.

The smile and wave of a hand when they see you from afar, or the fast walking of an enveloping hug to greet you, after a long absence. The forth coming of their presence when you desperately needed them, and seeming to just appear before you. The feeling of supernatural presence and the willing to help you any way they can.

This is the reason that there is Spirit in control of my life and my writings. Ella's Hand and Spirit: The aging yellow house on Route 119 at a place called Kelly Bottom, the house set close to the road.

This house being new to me as well as a month old second marriage. My understanding of the community and its people had yet to settle, in my mind, for this little town was unique in its presumptuous ways.

One night I was awaiting my husband Ralph to arrive from his flower distributing job, and I felt this cold rush of air pass by me. I was standing in the kitchen. Someone was definitely in the kitchen with me. I could feel the presence.

I continued to work on dinner. Again I felt the air. This time as if the warmth and cold blended. Then I saw her. This old women with grayish hair knotted up in a bun in the back of her head. There she stood with a look on her face as if to say, 69 DO YOU SEE ME OR NOT"? The flat of her hand lay against her cheek. Her appearance was short and nothing was said.

A few nights later. About 1:00 a.m. at a point in a miserable restless, no sleep night, I felt the presence again. The cold-warm air again.

The foot of the bed, there she stood... the old women appeared again as I sat bolt right up in bed. Ralph my husband did not awaken. This time the old women spoke. "Tell the Lynches I said hello." I have three Bible Verses for you. She proceeded to give me the scriptures and again disappeared.

The old women had one characteristic that stuck in my mind. She held her flat hand against her cheek. This would later cause me to find out who she was. I knew she was present in our house.

There was an antique four legged, squatty and heavily covered stool, which sat against the wall in the boy's room. The only way it creaked is when someone sat or stood on it. Many nights the boy's would complain that the stool creaked as if someone was rocking on it. Those same nights there was that cold warm air present.

Then one night she shockingly appeared in a rush. Strangely it was just two weeks before Ralph's father "BLINKER," passed away of Cancer of the Liver.

You see the old woman was Blinkers mother, ELLA, and Ralph's grandmother. Blinker was a devout and religious man.

It seems the family story goes, ELLA had a cancer on her on her cheek and the doctor tried to remove it and burnt her face and damaged the mussel in her cheek, thus the hand of Ella laid up her cheek because of pain. One knows the pain is always worse at night_ thus the rocking motion upon the stool late at night.

Somehow the old women came to me, because she knew I do not questions supernatural thing. Even the presence of God.

BROOKLYN FROLICS

by Susan C. Barto

Susan loved the sidewalks of New York. Brooklyn seemed the most perfect of all worlds to live in. She and her cousins reigned over the neighborhood—their throne being the old green bench in front of the two family house. She and her brother bill lived in the two family house with her cousins Andy, Claire and Merry. Another cousin Christine came to visit each weekend. Each day the neighborhood children gathered at the old green bench and played time, truth or consequences, and hide and seek. They listened for the ding of the good humor truck as good Uncle Joe bought ice cream for the whole neighborhood and kept mum so that they could indulge in another treat in the evening ALTHO they were only allowed good humor once a day.

Susan's closest friend of her heart was Bubbles, the daughter of a Rabbi who lived next door. Together they walked their doll carriages through the neighborhood and called each other sister. Susan had no other sister, but Bubbles and her cousins seemed as close to sisters as anyone could wish for. Real life began and ended on the streets of Brooklyn together with the neighborhood cronies. Years later when she read the peanuts cartoons, Susan was reminded of this. The screech sound that issued forth from adult mouths Susan agreed with. The only voices worth listening to were the voices of siblings and friends. Like Charles Schultz, Susan and her friends thought of adults as only shrill voices issuing from tall giants whose only purpose seemed to be to annoy and get in the way of the children's fun.

Susan's favorite excursion consisted of a trip to the library that included crossing the wide traffic filled ocean parkway with its bicycle paths and walking paths where young mamas pushed their opulent baby carriages. After crossing ocean parkway that sometimes was strewn with horse chestnuts from the horseback riding crowd, she passed the chicken slaughter house with her eyes averted and passed the dry cleaners where Hitler hung in effigy. After passing these sights the library came into view, and for an hour or so Susan lost herself in the sights and smells of the library-the smell of the books and the library paste, the look of the stacks and rows of books stacked so neatly on the shelves. She chose her newest Mary POPPINS or Betsy, TACY, and TIBB, and cradled the books in her arms as she wended her way back home to the stoop and the old green bench. She could not read on the bench, however, too many distractions from the other children. She read on her bed at night. Her home was filled with turbulent arguments between her parents, and the books served to drown out the reality and transport her to other worlds. Something reading managed to do for Susan for the rest of her life.

Susan's father surprised her with a dollhouse big enough to enter and equip with her dolls and doll carriages and doll furniture. She and Bubbles filled with glee put their dolls and things in the dollhouse and went to the store to buy crepe paper to make curtains for the dollhouse. When they returned she discovered that Billy had converted the dollhouse into a clubhouse and a clubhouse unfortunately, for Susan , it remained. However, as a clubhouse it was enjoyed by the entire neighborhood and on it they climbed via the lilac bush to the roof of the clubhouse and from there to the roofs of the neighborhood garages. They could leap from one roof to another—kings of the world and the neighborhood they believed themselves to be and indeed until they were called in for lunch or dinner they were.

School proved to be a pleasant addition to neighborhood life. The grade school—P.S. 215—around the corner from their house and next to a candy store-seemed like one more adventure in Susan's life to be savored and enjoyed.

She could already read, and she promptly skipped the first grade going from kindergarten to second grade in one leap. On the way home the children stopped in at the candy store where they bought school supplies and had their choice of penny candy arranged in a colorful array. The hard part to Susan,choosing which candies on which to spend her pennies, engaged her each afternoon. Homework proved to be easy or non existent, and life on the street engaged the children. Stoop ball, stick ball, bouncing the spalding pink balls and turning their knees over the ball used countless hours. Bouncing the ball to the tune of sidewalks of New York, Susan loved this life.

When the time came for her to learn to roller skate, Andy grabbed her one morning when she came onto the street and put the skates on her feet. "Today, Susan, you learn to roller skate." Since Andy was boss, Susan skated. Riding the two wheeler proved to be the same formula. No one ever heard of training wheels. Andy said, "today you ride the two wheeler/ and Susan rode. She fell off into a bramble bush at the end of the street, got back on the bike scratched and a bit bloody, but brave enough to ride back home on the two wheeler. 'BRAVO', Andy cried.

Life tumbled on in this agreeable fashion on the streets of Brooklyn until Susan hit eight years old. At that time her father moved her family to a gorgeous house on a tree lined street in the suburb of summit, new jersey. Susan experienced a trauma from which she never completely recovered. Forever, her heart would beat faster when she arrived in the city. However, she relished visits to and from Brooklyn, and the Brooklyn frolics she had experienced in her first eight years remained with her always. East side, west side all around the town. The tots played ring around rosy London bridge is falling down. Boys and girls together. Me and MAMIE O'ROURKE. We tripped the life fantastic on the sidewalks of New York.

SNOW AND FRIENDSHIP REACHES BEYOND THE EVERY DAY JOURNEY

by Juliet Rhodes Lynch

The sky is a mist of gray-- --darker gray with Gunboat gray blobbed in patches. The thickness of smudges, in the early dawn of daylight, softness yet the depths of sadness's. The feeling of doom and gloom shoots into ones emotions. In the corners of the sky you can see a whiteness that seems to be pushing the dark clouds together into a pattern of puffs, pouched out. I, feel a tingle of cold, which flings more tingles as it pelters rain drops down upon the ground. Within several minutes the droplet become white feather looking objects that form into CRYSTAL SNOW FLAKES.

Some people journey out their doors to feel the temperature and check to see the outer weight of a coats and outerwear to put on. Wondering if the need for boots and umbrella is needed,

The decisions of """" oh, my gosh, it couldn't have snowed that much in just a few minutes. Now the race is on to call to the office or school or husbands work to see what is to be the plan of the day for all concerned? There is a fast thought as to gathering whatever is needed for a safety bag for the car and emergency supplies also, Flashlight, matches, blankets, bottled water, non-perishable food, extra clothes. Note book to write out information that might be needed and a map and high-lighter pen as well as regular ink pen.

Thoughts of older people who live nearby and even some older family members , who live in other areas, Young people waking up to hearing no school and grinning from ear to ear. Trying to finding warm layered clothes to put on. Then heading out into the snow, to enjoy the day and new adventures and experiences.

Walking out the front door a neighbor has walked partially up the front snow covered walk, and greets me with a smile and a cup of hot chocolate. I laugh an asked what he was doing out in this crazy weather. We watched the snow being crazy and laughed at how much snow had come down since we had gotten up this particular morning. I had a silly giddy feeling as if my childhood had grabbed me and slammed me down on the ground and I was laughing almost uncontrollable. Several people in the neighborhood walking over to see what was going on and we all started to laugh and I was laughing so hard I couldn't even get up from the 3 feet of snow that had fallen. Someone reached down to help me up and I ended up pulling them down also and they had grabbed someone else's arm as they slid down. It caused a chain reaction and the next thing I saw was a couple of people doing SNOW ANGELS, throwing snow balls and building a snowman.

CHILDREN? NO! these Adults laughing and having the time of their lives, and shortly there were children rolling out into the snow too. WHAT'S THIS? No cell phones, no electronics', and a enter reaction with adults, dogs bouncing around and barking. Plastic sleds and old time sleds had been found way back in people's garages. What has overcome these people and what has happened to the neighborhood? There were some new people who walked over and joined in the fun too.

Pretty soon someone suggested we go over to the vacant land on the corner, which belonged to the neighborhood for later construction of an area for kids to play ball and have for some sports games. The idea grew into having a bonfire and marshmallows, hot dogs, coffee and hot chocolate and whatever could be found sit on and to wrap around us to keep warm as we gathered around the bon-fire. We all got excited and gathered things up and brought to the area.

Somehow I felt that softness of what I remembered from the old days when I was a kid. I felt tears falling down my cheeks and realize I wasn't by myself in these emotions. A couple of people started to sing in gentle voices some songs from our childhood pasts. I began to realize that somehow the people who we hardly ever saw, but waved to were delightful people and that we were having great fun and special memory making experiences that would last as friendships and actual experiencing what being neighbors really meant. Later, there was a time of shoveling the snow and helping each other with things that hadn't been done because there was a lack of people to help do them. Who'd a known they were right here in our neighborhood. It didn't stop there, as there was a church nearby and even the pastor had join in the gathering and invited anyone who would like to have a church to come to, was surely welcome to come to his church. Friendships were formed and church services were attended and kids found new friends. THIS WASN'T AN EVERY DAY JOURNEY…BUT, CRYSTAL SNOW FLAKES CAUSED A BEAUTIFUL DAY AND NEW DELIGHTFUL PEOPLE TO COME INTO OUR LIVES.

1] You must be 18 years or have parent/guardian consent.

2] You must reside in the USA / Canada.

3] You must submit your own original unpublished poem and/or stories.

4] Submissions must be typed on a single sheet of white paper (one side only, no color, no onion skin.)

5] Your complete legal name, address must appear in upper right-hand corner of the page.

6] Only three submissions per envelope, NO entry fee.

7] Winners will be determined by Publisher selection. All awarded prizes are final.

8] Amount of prize is based on number of entries received.

9] Deadline for entry is the 15th of first month issue's per quarter.

John Doe
1234 Helm St.
Maxwell, KY 12345

Poem Title

This is where
The body of
Your poem
Should
Reside.

Any Style,
Any Subject
Any Genre

Your Name Here

Sample Poem Submission:

8.5"   11"

John Doe
1234 Helm St.
Maxwell, KY 12345

Story Title
Your Name

The manuscript should be clearly typed, single-spaced, double-spaced between paragraphs or stanzas, on white medium-weight paper. Do not use ornamental type, justified right margins, or hyphenated words. Do not use liquid paper to correct errors on your submission. Sheets should be of

Sample Poem Submission:

8.5"

GUIDELINES

$0 No reading fees for submission to Anthologies, The Drury Gazette or Theo's Compass. Submission does not guarantee acceptance nor publishing of submitted work. An Author Release Form must accompany ALL Submissions. Submission will ONLY be acknowledged or returned if providing a S.A.S.E. (Self-Addressed-Stamped-Envelope) with proper postage. Always check with the publisher for most current guidelines with a query letter.

Submissions may be Any Subject, Any Style, And Any Genre. Typed. Some restrictions may apply. You are NEVER under ANY obligation to purchase anything at any time. Purchasers are given premium consideration and placement. You may receive offers to purchase publications or services however you are NOT obligated NOR required to buy anything to guarantee publication of accepted work. Whether you purchase or not accepted work is still published.

Accepted submissions will be typed set, a publisher proof mailed to the legal originator for correction of possible errors. Should originator not return publisher proof within the time frame given work will be published "AS IS". ONLY typesetting errors may be corrected at that time. Publisher Proofs are the sole and complete property of the Publisher and MUST be returned.

Submissions are NOT open to the public at large. You must have received a direct mail invitation or been recommended by a past or present author to have your submission considered. If you are submitting an unsolicited manuscript it is required you state the author/publication recommending or sponsoring you. These are Not-For-Profit publications. Supported by my personal funds. Donations or purchases aid in offsetting the associated cost. Submissions NOT adhering to these conditions will be rejected.

The sole purpose of Anthologies, The Drury Gazette, and Theo's Compass is to help authors with limited to no means promote their material. No commercial adverts support or are present in these publications. Included adverts are FREE to book advertisements for authors and FREE or EXCHANGED adverts of publications whose goals are similar.

Anthologies: Every accepted author has their work published for FREE which includes their photo and BIO. The Drury Gazette & Theo's Compass: Every accepted author has his or her work published for FREE, sometimes includes photo and BIO, and the author receives FREE advert space to promote their published book, music, and film or solicited orders. All adverts are the sole and complete responsibility of the advertising party.

* S.A.S.E. = Self-Addressed-Stamped-Envelope
** (Nothing Pornographic)
*** Author may retract submission at any time in writing prior to typesetting or mailed publisher proofs; whichever comes first. No retraction will be accepted if either of these conditions exists without compensation to the publisher for time, expense and delays. Removal requires both author and publisher written agreement.
**** Any use in whole or in part of my copyright material in print or electronically is NOT authorized without my express written consent. Any such use in any published form whether you receive payment or not is strictly prohibited and must monetarily compensate me for such use. You must cease and desist immediately.

IMPORTANT: Author should retain a complete photocopy of the manuscript, not only to facilitate correspondence between editor and author but to serve as insurance against loss of original copy. The Drury Gazette is usually very careful not to lose or damage the manuscript, but my legal responsibility does not extend beyond "reasonable care." Everyone that meets requirements is welcome to submit poems of reasonable length, any style, and any subject matter. There are no fees of any kind to have your poem published if accepted. Any submission may be removed at any time prior to typesetting or mailed galleys. After such time without a substantial valid reason, the author agrees to remit payment to the publisher for the cost of typesetting, galleys, and publishing delays. I reserve the exclusive right to reject any submission without notice for any reason whatsoever. Author release and submission forms available online at

www.druryspublishing.com

Note: Unless specified otherwise - submissions will not be returned. *Poems/Stories should be typed as the example shown above.*

Use of profanity or patently vulgar language — Using language that is racist, hateful, sexual, discriminating or obscene in nature is strictly prohibited and will not be tolerated.

The Drury Gazette™

$0 No reading fees for submission to Anthologies, The Drury Gazette or Theo's Compass. Submission does not guarantee acceptance nor publishing of submitted work. An Author Release Form must accompany ALL Submissions. Submission will ONLY be acknowledged or returned if providing a S.A.S.E. (Self-Addressed-Stamped-Envelope) with proper postage.

Submissions may be Any Subject, Any Style, And Any Genre. Typed. Some restrictions may apply. You are NEVER under ANY obligation to purchase anything at any time. Purchasers are given premium consideration and placement. You may receive offers to purchase publications or services however you are NOT obligated NOR required to buy anything to guarantee publication of accepted work. Whether you purchase or not accepted work is still published.

Accepted submissions will be typed set, a publisher proof mailed to the legal originator for correction of possible errors. Should originator not return publisher proof within the time frame given work will be published "AS IS". ONLY typesetting errors may be corrected at that time. Publisher Proofs are the sole and complete property of the Publisher and MUST be returned.

Submissions are NOT open to the public at large. You must have received a direct mail invitation or been recommended by a past or present author to have your submission considered. If you are submitting an unsolicited manuscript it is required you state the author/publication recommending or sponsoring you. These are Not-For-Profit publications. Supported by my personal funds. Donations or purchases aid in offsetting the associated cost. Submissions NOT adhering to these conditions will be rejected.

The sole purpose of Anthologies, The Drury Gazette, and Theo's Compass is to help authors with limited to no means promote their material. No commercial adverts support or are present in these publications. Included adverts are FREE to book advertisements for authors and FREE or EXCHANGED adverts of publications whose goals are similar.

Anthologies: Every accepted author has their work published for FREE which includes their photo and BIO. The Drury Gazette & Theo's Compass: Every accepted author has his or her work published for FREE, sometimes includes photo and BIO, and the author receives FREE advert space to promote their published book, music, and film or solicited orders. All adverts are the sole and complete responsibility of the advertising party.

Fighting Chance

Fighting Chance is a magazine which features: fantasy, dark fantasy, horror, science fiction, adventure stories, short one-act plays, short-shorts, and poetry.

Love's Chance

Love's Chance is a magazine which features Love and Romance -prose and poetry.

Each magazine will be published annually. There will be a new, expanded format. Single copies are $5.00 per issue. A three-year subscription is $12.00.

Send payment for subscription or individual copies to: Suzerain Enterprises c/o Milton Kerr P. O. Box 60336 Worcester, MA 01606

Guidelines for Authors

Short stories up to 2,000 words - submit one at a time. Poetry not to exceed 20 lines - submit no more than three at any one time. Short-shorts (to 500 words) - submit one at a time.

Submit only camera ready text (no handwriting or page numbers) with author's name following the end of the piece. Use white paper only - any other color will be rejected.

There are no reading fees; there are no payments. Previously published works and simultaneous submissions are okay.

Include SASE with all submissions - otherwise, they will not be returned. The same goes for query letters. No SASE; no response.

Send complete manuscript and/or payment for subscription or individual copies to: Suzerain Enterprises c/o Milton Kerr P. O. Box 60336 Worcester, MA 01606

September Sentiments

EAN13: 9781453653913 Page Count: 104 Binding Type: US Trade Paper Trim Size: 6" x 9" Language: English Color: Black and White Related Categories: Poetry / General. Find it available wherever fine books are sold. Check with your local book store or favorite online bookstore.

www.ingramcontent.com/pod-product-compliance
Lightning Source LLC
Chambersburg PA
CBHW080818250626
47159CB00010B/3430

9780692658420